Wings Across the Moon

by Linda Hargrove
pictures by Joung Un Kim

HarperFestival®
A Division of HarperCollins Publishers

Twilight,
Near night,
See the rising moon.

First chance,
Wings dance,
Black against the moon.

Whose wings?

Moth's wings,
Flutter, hum, and whir.

Whose wings?

Goose's wings,
Whistle, whoosh, and furl.

Whose wings?

Cricket's wings,
Fiddle, chirp, and chirr.

Starlight,
Dark night,
A still quiet moon.

Night sky,
Wings fly,
Swiftly 'cross the moon.

Whose wings?
Firefly's wings,
Glimmer, glow, and hide.

Whose wings?

Bat's wings,
Dart, dip, and dive.

Whose wings?

Owl's wings,
Lift, swoop, and glide.

Moonlight,
Calm night,
A warm peaceful room.